This book belongs to

Olivia

Happy 1st Birthday 🎂

Love Uncle Tommy & Aunt Jodi

Published by Advance Publishers

© 1998 Disney Enterprises, Inc.

Written by Lisa Ann Marsoli
Illustrated by Dean Kleven, Orlando de la Paz, and Brad McMahon
Produced by Bumpy Slide Books

ISBN: 1-57973-006-X

10 9 8 7 6 5 4 3 2 1

DISNEY'S
POCAHONTAS

AN UNLIKELY PAIR

Meeko the raccoon didn't much like dogs. The only one he knew was a pug named Percy, who was spoiled and awfully unfriendly. Percy was used

to living on a ship with lots of people, so he didn't
know how to act around other animals.

Now Percy lived on land, in a new world. He was causing Pocahontas, Meeko, and Flit all kinds of trouble.

One day he got into the village's food supply and nibbled half the kernels off every ear of corn.

"You mustn't go around taking whatever you want," Pocahontas told him patiently. "We would be happy to share our food with you, but you need to share with us, too."

Then the pug took to napping in the hut where Pocahontas and her father, Chief Powhatan, lived. He always seemed to be sleeping exactly where the chief wanted to sit.

Chief Powhatan had not wanted to allow the dog inside, but he had agreed to it to make Pocahontas happy. Little by little, however, the chief's patience was wearing thin.

"Pocahontas!" he called one day, when the pug was spread across his bench. "Get this animal out of here!"

The others in the village weren't too happy about their new visitor, either. Shut out of Chief Powhatan's hut, Percy whined and howled at night. Soon the wolves in the surrounding woods answered his calls, raising a deafening din. In the morning, the bleary-eyed villagers complained because they had not been able to sleep.

"Pocahontas," Chief Powhatan said sternly, "it's time that dog went to live in the forest with the other animals."

"But Father," Pocahontas protested, "Percy is used to being taken care of. He doesn't know how to survive on his own."

"Then it is time for him to learn," the chief answered.

Pocahontas knew from the tone of her father's voice that there was no sense in arguing. His mind was made up.

That very day, Pocahontas took Percy deep
into the forest and shooed him away. As always,
Meeko was by her side.

"Please keep an eye on him," Pocahontas said
to her friend. "He's going to need help."

Then, before Percy could turn to follow her,
Pocahontas disappeared into the trees.

But Meeko didn't care about Percy. He was
wondering where he might find a tasty midmorning
snack. He began to dig with his sharp claws, never
even noticing the chubby pug following him.

Sometimes Percy had a hard time keeping up, but he managed to keep Meeko in sight as the raccoon darted under leaves, through bushes, and over fallen trees. Percy didn't get along with Meeko, but at least his was a familiar face!

For several days, the pug watched Meeko
and did whatever the raccoon did. Soon Percy, too,
could find nuts and berries and wild vegetables.

He even learned how to cross a stream by scrambling across the rocks — a big accomplishment, since he was afraid of the water!

One afternoon Pocahontas and Nakoma went for a walk in the forest, hoping to see how Percy was adjusting to life in the wild. How happy Pocahontas was to discover Percy and Meeko snoozing in opposite ends of a hollow log.

Pocahontas smiled. "Wouldn't it be funny," she said to Nakoma, "if those two were actually starting to like each other?"

Meeko and Percy were awakened by the sound
of the two girls laughing.

"Come on, you two!" Pocahontas called. "Take
a walk with us! It's a shame to sleep such a beautiful
day away!"

Always ready for adventure, Meeko darted after them — then stopped to make sure Percy was following.

Soon Meeko began to think of lunch. He was
a lucky raccoon, indeed, for up ahead he caught a
whiff of something sweet and delicious. He followed
the scent to the mouth of a cave, where he found a
bush full of fat, juicy blackberries. Moments later,
Percy was sharing the sticky feast.

Pocahontas and Nakoma looked around. "Did you see where Meeko and Percy went?" Pocahontas asked.

"Don't worry," Nakoma reassured her. "They're probably just having fun."

Meeko and Percy weren't the only creatures
looking for lunch in the forest that afternoon. As
they licked the sticky berry juice from their paws,
they were startled by a loud rustling in the cave.
Soon three black noses poked their way out of the

darkness — three black noses attached to three hungry baby bears!

Meeko was smart enough to know not to tangle with bears, no matter how small. He backed away slowly. But not Percy. He stood frozen in fear.

Then they heard a growl. It was fierce and
low and very, very close. The bears' mother had
returned, and she was not happy to see visitors
so close to her cubs. She reared up menacingly
on her hind legs.

But when Meeko turned to run away, he got his foot caught in a vine.

The mother bear reached for Meeko, but Percy
barked wildly and raced between her legs. She
answered him with a series of loud, terrifying growls.

"Do you hear that?" Pocahontas cried.
"Meeko and Percy are in trouble. Let's go!"
    She and Nakoma raced through the forest,
following the spine-chilling sounds.

By the time the girls reached the scene, Percy had managed to lure the mother bear away from Meeko. Nakoma and Pocahontas freed the raccoon, then called to the dog.

"Percy! Come here!" Pocahontas called.

The pug raced over to his friends, his short legs moving as fast as they could. The four escaped into the trees while the mother bear went to join her babies.

"Some quiet walk in the woods that turned out to be!" Pocahontas exclaimed. She and Nakoma collapsed onto a soft bed of pine needles to catch their breath. "Honestly, you two, how did —" She looked around. "Meeko? Percy?"

"Over there," Nakoma said, pointing.
Behind a rock, Percy and Meeko pressed close
to each other, trembling with fear.
"It's all right now," Pocahontas reassured them.

Back at the village, Pocahontas and Nakoma
told everyone of Meeko and Percy's adventure. No
one could believe that the spoiled, helpless dog had
survived one of nature's most fearsome creatures.

"Not only that," insisted Pocahontas, "but he saved Meeko's life as well. I don't know what would have happened to all of us if Percy hadn't distracted the mother bear."

And so it was decided that a ceremony would be held to make Percy a special mascot of Powhatan's tribe. That night, as a fire glowed, Percy was decorated with feathers and face paint.

"Perhaps we were too hasty in judging our friend," the chief proclaimed. "All creatures can change — once nature provides them with the opportunity."

From that day on, Meeko looked forward to spending time together with Percy. The strange visitor from another land had become his trusted

friend. And while it was true that Meeko had taught
an old dog some new tricks, that little raccoon had
learned a few things himself.

Percy was a nuisance —
He was spoiled to the bone.
But one day it was time for him
To strike out on his own.
Now he takes care of himself,
And cares for others, too.
He knows if you try hard enough
There's nothing you can't do!